Lizzie McGuire

Lizzie Goes Wild

W9-BMR-799

Adapted by Kirsten Larsen

Based on the series created by Terri Minsky

New York

Copyright © 2002 Disney Enterprises, Inc.

All rights reserved. No part of this book may be reproduced
or transmitted in any form or by any means, electronic or
mechanical, including photocopying, recording, or by any
information storage and retrieval system, without written
permission from the publisher. For information address
Disney Press, 114 Fifth Avenue, New York, New York 10011-5690.

Printed in the United States of America

First Edition
1 3 5 7 9 10 8 6 4 2

Library of Congress Catalog Card Number: 2002101297

ISBN 0-7868-4540-6
For more Disney Press fun, visit www.disneybooks.com
Visit ZoogDisney.com

If you purchased this book without a cover, you should be aware
that this book is stolen property. It was reported as "unsold and
destroyed" to the publisher, and neither the author nor the
publisher has received any payment for this "stripped" book.

PART ONE

CHAPTER ONE

"If train A and train B are traveling at different speeds, heading for the same destination, and train A is traveling at ninety miles an hour. . . ."

Okay, Mrs. Wortman is a little too excited about math for a Monday morning, Lizzie McGuire thought, as she watched her teacher's shiny black hair swing from side to side. Bits of chalk flew from her hand as she scribbled the equation on the blackboard. She looked like an actress in a TV commercial for overexcited algebra teachers who use conditioner.

Lizzie stifled a yawn, then copied the problem into her sparkly notebook with her purple fuzzy pencil. Train A = 90 mph, she wrote. She stared at the equation, wishing that she felt some of Mrs. Wortman's love of the word problem. Then she drew a little train and a conductor with an *A* on his cap. Next she drew her best friends, Miranda and Gordo, riding in the cars and a picture of herself hanging off the caboose, waving to . . . to whom? Lizzie thought for a moment. Then she added Ethan Craft, the cutest boy in the eighth grade, waving back to her from the depot. Was Ethan sad? Why, yes, he was! Lizzie decided. She added a thought bubble over Ethan's head. "Yo! Don't leave me, Lizzie! I love you!" she wrote inside it. *Now* she was wide-awake!

Unless i'm on the train and it's taking me and my friends to a private rock concert, i'm just not that interested.

Suddenly, Lizzie heard the kids around her snicker. Instinctively, she covered her notebook, but Miranda clued her in by pointing to the desk behind Lizzie's. It belonged to Angel Lieberman, tormentor extraordinaire. Lizzie turned around just in time to see Angel quickly pull her hand away from Lizzie's hair.

Lizzie stared at her. Angel had the worst reputation in the whole school. In fact, she looked exactly like the girl pictured on the cover of those "Do you know who their friends are?" warning pamphlets Hillridge

Junior High School sent home to parents year after year. Her hair stuck straight up from her head in spiky purple and blue ponytails. She wore a ratty fake-fur vest over her gray ribbed shirt, and her eyes were thickly lined in black. Stuck to the tip of her thumb was a bright pink wad of bubble gum. Angel smiled innocently at Lizzie and popped the gum back into her mouth. She would be so much nicer if she bathed, Lizzie thought, wrinkling her nose and facing forward.

A second later, Lizzie felt a tap on her shoulder, and she turned back around. Angel had turned her eyelids inside out and was rolling her eyes back in her head.

"Gross!" Lizzie whispered.

"I know you are, Frizzie McGuire," Angel replied, just loud enough for Mrs. Wortman to hear. But before Lizzie could explain the vast difference between frizzy hair and purposely crimped hair, the teacher spun around.

"Ms. Lieberman, is there a problem?" Mrs. Wortman asked.

"No," Angel said quickly.

Mrs. Wortman looked at Lizzie. "Ms. McGuire, problem?"

Lizzie looked down at her notebook. "No."

"Good," Mrs. Wortman said, turning back to the blackboard. "So, if train B has traveled one hundred twenty-two miles at sixty miles per hour. . . ."

Lizzie went back to taking notes. But in a moment she felt something wet on the back of her neck. She reached up and found—Angel's chewed bubble gum!

"Oh, gross!" Lizzie groaned.

Angel leaned forward in her seat. "Oh, I'm sorry, Frizzie," she whispered with a sneer. "I thought you were my desk."

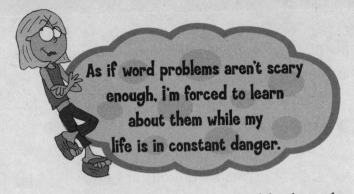

As if word problems aren't scary enough, i'm forced to learn about them while my life is in constant danger.

Lizzie shot Miranda a panicked look as she tried to pull Angel's A.B.C. gum out of her purposely crimped (i.e., *not* frizzy) hair. As usual, Mrs. Wortman had no idea her class had derailed. She was happily chugging along on the B train.

Then Angel coughed. "Boring!" The class burst out laughing.

Mrs. Wortman whirled around, her shiny hair neatly following. "That's it!" she snapped. "Clear your desks except for a pencil." She grabbed a stack of quizzes from her desk and began passing them out. "Write your name on the upper right-hand corner of your papers and show all of your work," Mrs. Wortman instructed.

"Great. A pop quiz," Miranda said grimly as she closed her notebook and placed it on the floor.

"I love the smell of pop quizzes in the morning," Gordo added sarcastically.

Angel rolled her eyes in disgust. "What planet are you from again?" she asked him. "Gor-dork?"

Lizzie chose to ignore them, be a good student, and read the first problem. *The Johnsons are trying to build a patio around their pool. If they want their patio to be twenty feet long and fourteen feet wide, and the pool is twelve feet long and eight feet wide, how many square feet of wood will they need to build the patio?* Lizzie freaked for a second. Who are the Johnsons, when did they get a pool, and why wasn't I invited to their pool party? she wondered.

Lizzie quickly shook those thoughts out of her head and focused on the quiz. She breathed a sigh of relief. She knew how to solve it. All she had to do was subtract the area of the pool from the area of the patio. Unlike some people (who wear too much eyeliner), she'd done her homework the night before, thank you very much. Lizzie quickly finished the problem and moved on to the next question. This quiz was going to be EZ.

Just then, out of the corner of her eye, Lizzie noticed Angel leaning over her shoulder, trying to see her paper.

"Stop it!" Lizzie whispered, covering her answers with her arm.

"Let me see your paper!" Angel demanded.

"No! Cheater!" Lizzie glanced over at Mrs. Wortman, who was strolling between the desks at the far side of the room.

"Are you afraid Mrs. Wortman will see?" Angel taunted.

"I'm so *not* afraid," Lizzie snapped back, barely managing to keep her voice to a whisper.

"Prove it," Angel said. "Let me see."

"What part of 'no' don't you understand?" Lizzie asked.

Angel leaned back in her seat and folded her arms. "Coward," she scoffed and then she kicked the back of Lizzie's chair. Hard.

Lizzie glared at Angel. But Angel just smiled, her arms still crossed against her chest. She's so not going to leave me alone until she gets what she wants, Lizzie realized. Pursing her lips, Lizzie casually tilted her paper so Angel could copy it. And she did. Angel copied and copied and copied for what felt like forever. Finally, trying to speed her along, Lizzie tapped her fuzzy purple pencil directly at an answer.

"Ladies!" Lizzie jumped at the sound of Mrs. Wortman's sharp voice. She looked up to see her math teacher standing right over her desk. Mrs. Wortman was glaring down at them both. "I don't tolerate cheating," she said, snatching their quizzes. "You can finish up your conversation in detention."

Lizzie gasped. Cheating? I wasn't cheating, she thought, I was being cheated on! And did she just say the D-word? Lizzie's heart began to pound, and the room started to spin.

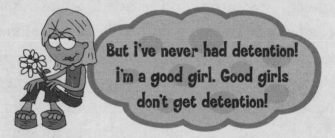

But i've never had detention! i'm a good girl. Good girls don't get detention!

When Lizzie finally managed to catch her breath, she realized everyone was staring at her, including Gordo and Miranda. But Angel didn't seem upset at all. She just crossed her arms, playfully kicked at Lizzie's seat, and smiled.

"Well, Frizzie McGuire, welcome to my world," she whispered. "See you in detention."

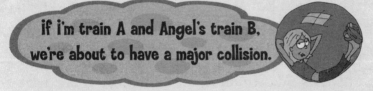

if i'm train A and Angel's train B, we're about to have a major collision.

All through Language Arts, Lizzie worried about what Mrs. Wortman must think of her now. She decided to write her a little note explaining what had happened. Then it came to her. It would be so much cuter to compose it as a word problem.

If one of Mrs. Wortman's best and most trusted students got caught cheating for the first time, how long would it take Mrs. Wortman to trust her again?

Okay, sweet, but it showed zero under-standing of algebra. Lizzie tried another.

If student B+ (who always did her home-work) were taking a quiz, how long before student F (who never did her homework) would try to cheat off student B+?

Perfect! But as Lizzie added drawings to help Mrs. Wortman distinguish between student B+ and student F, she started to get angry. I'm one of Mrs. Wortman's best and most trusted B+ students, Lizzie thought, and she blames *me* for cheating? Lizzie threw the note into the trash, sat back in her chair, crossed her arms across her chest, and glared at the ceiling. She couldn't wait for this day to be over.

But when the final bell rang, Lizzie knew it rang for her.

As everyone else ran for the exit doors, Lizzie stood beside Gordo and Miranda, staring at a door marked DETENTION. Resigned to do the time, Lizzie reached for the knob, but a boy in a black T-shirt shoved past her.

He scowled at Lizzie, then kicked open the door and walked through.

Lizzie looked at her friends. "Isn't this when you offer me some comfort? Guidance? Anything?" she cried. "I'm so going to get killed if I go in there."

"Um . . ." Gordo said.

"Don't look anybody in the eye?" Miranda suggested.

Lizzie watched as the door opened again. Her eyes went wide. Did she just hear a scream from inside?

"It's just detention, right?" she said, trying to make herself feel better. "I mean, everyone in there can't be a criminal. *I* got detention. I'm sure there'll be at least one other normal person in there."

"That depends on how you define *normal*," Gordo told her. "We all thought Eli Saxon was normal."

"Until he ate his shoes," Miranda added.

They are *not* helping Lizzie thought.

"Just try to blend in," Gordo coached Lizzie. "Act tough."

"Tough?" Lizzie looked at him in disbelief. "Gordo, this is *me* you're talking to."

Just then, Angel walked up. She silently stared Lizzie down as she yanked the detention door open and walked inside. As the door closed behind her, Lizzie shuddered. No doubt about it, this time she *definitely* heard a scream.

Miranda patted Lizzie's shoulder. "We'll remember you fondly," she said. Lizzie took a deep breath and walked through the door.

On the other side of freedom, she paused at the doorway and looked around. Three or four kids were in the middle of a spitball fight. (It was hard to tell about the fourth—she seemed completely unaware of the spitballs hanging from her hair.) The black-T-shirt kid was slumped in his seat, drawing a skull and crossbones on his arm with a ballpoint pen. At the front of the room, the school's drama teacher sat perched on the edge of a desk, reading a stack of papers. As Lizzie walked up to him, she wondered what he had done wrong to get stuck in here.

"Um, hi. I'm Lizzie McGuire," she said hesitantly. "I'm, uh, here for detention?"

The teacher glanced up. "Ah, a fresh face. How entertaining for the others," he said. He gave her a tight little smile, seemingly oblivious of the crumpled balls of paper that soared past his head. "Welcome, Miss McGuire. A hearty welcome. Please, take a seat." He gestured grandly toward a row of desks. Lizzie hesitated, not wanting to sit near *any* of her fellow detentionites. "I don't care which one," the teacher told her. "I really don't."

Lizzie took a seat at the front of the room.

Cautiously, she glanced over her shoulder to the back rows where the rest of the kids were sitting. What's with bad kids and back rows? Lizzie thought, and then realized that all those bad kids were staring back at her. Pretending to scratch an itch on her cheek with her shoulder, she quickly turned back around.

Just then the teacher stood up. "Okay, people," he said loudly. Everyone but Lizzie ignored him. "I'm excusing myself for no more than five minutes. That should give me enough time to make copies of my play, which is a work of genius that I don't expect you little monkeys to understand." The teacher looked around the room and shook his head in disgust.

Lizzie stared at him in horror. The teacher was leaving her all alone with the future occupants of cell block C? She needed his protection. She couldn't let him go. Lizzie desperately racked her brain for something to say. But as he walked to the door, Lizzie noticed that someone had taped a KICK ME, I'M DRAMATIC sign to his back. He couldn't protect her, Lizzie thought; it was totally up to her now.

As soon as the door shut behind him, the room went crazy. One girl flicked the lights on and off. A boy jumped from desktop to desktop. Another boy and girl ripped the pages out of an English textbook and made paper airplanes. The black-T-shirt kid picked up a smaller boy and hung him on a coat hook in the back of the room. Lizzie gripped the edge of her desk as though it were her only ally.

Just then she saw Angel Lieberman coming toward her. Angel's eyes were narrowed into little slits, and her hands were balled into fists. "I was supposed to be the first one in line to buy the next Eminem CD," she hissed. "Then you had to go and open your big mouth just because I wanted to cheat off your paper."

Lizzie glanced around the room, but there was no way out. Two kids were arm wrestling in front of the door. It was her worst nightmare realized. Yes, even worse than the one involving splitting her pants in front of Ethan Craft. She was actually trapped in an unsupervised classroom with an angry Angel Lieberman.

Lizzie needed a plan. Fast.

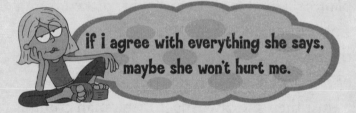

Lizzie looked Angel in the eye and shrugged her shoulders. "Maybe you're right," she said coolly. "It was just a stupid pop quiz. I should have just let you cheat. Next time we have a test, my answers are your answers." She smiled at Angel, hoping she looked friendly.

Still alive.
Seems to be working.

Angel eyed Lizzie suspiciously. "You're really going to let me cheat?" she asked.

"I guess so," Lizzie replied, thinking promises made in lockdown weren't exactly promises. Suddenly, to Lizzie's surprise, Angel plopped down in the seat next to her.

"Frizzie McGuire, I misjudged you," she said. "I may even let you join my band."

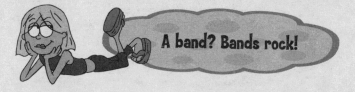

A band? Bands rock!

"You have a band?" Lizzie asked, trying not to sound overly excited.

"Not yet," Angel told her. "But one day I'm

gonna make some music and travel the world. Go my own way."

"Sounds really cool," Lizzie admitted.

"Yup." Angel nodded. "Just me, my music, and my fans. That's the only way to L-squared."

"L-squared?" Lizzie asked.

"Two L's," Angel explained. She held up her left thumb and index finger in an L shape. "Live Large. You know, go where the wind blows me."

Lizzie nodded. Talking with Angel was easier than she thought.

Angel's not scary— she's misunderstood.

"So, why'd you sit down next to me?" Lizzie asked.

Angel rolled her eyes. "Look around," she

said. "Like I'm really going to spend my valuable detention time talking to this bunch of double-E's."

Lizzie thought hard, then bit her lip. "What's a double-E?" She hated to ask.

Angel rolled her eyes again, annoyed. "How many Es are there in 'geek'?" she asked Lizzie.

"Two," Lizzie answered.

"And in 'dweeb'?"

"Two. Oh!" Lizzie said, suddenly getting it. "Double-E's. Geeks and dweebs. That's pretty good."

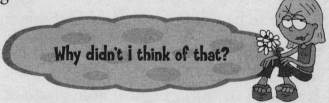

Why didn't i think of that?

Lizzie smiled. This detention thing was turning out to be *very* educational in the school of cool.

CHAPTER TWO

"Aaaaah!" Lizzie screamed as she walked into her house. She figured her mom would be waiting for her, but she didn't expect her mom to be waiting *right behind the front door.*

"You're late."

Hands on her hips, Lizzie's mom glared at her daughter. Lizzie stood just inside the doorway, clutching her books and shifting uneasily from foot to foot. Outside the windows she could see the streetlights coming on.

"I know. Sorry, Mom," Lizzie said lightly, trying to get past her mother.

Mrs. McGuire stared at her daughter in disbelief. "Sorry? 'Sorry,' you say? What could you have possibly been doing that you couldn't take *one minute* to call me!"

This probably wasn't a good time to once again beg for that cell phone, Lizzie thought. Her mom should really understand that finding a public phone at school that actually worked and wasn't covered in sticky, germy who-knows-what takes more than *one minute*.

"Well?" Mrs. McGuire snapped.

Lizzie prepared to tell her. She always told her mom everything, and her mom always understood. Eventually. But how could she possibly explain being afraid of a girl named *Angel*, failing a math quiz because she didn't want any more gum in her hair, how Mrs. Wortman should have understood, since she obviously really likes *her* own hair, too. . . .

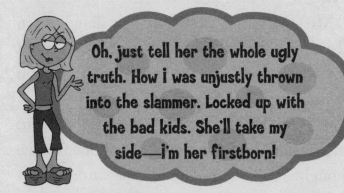

Oh, just tell her the whole ugly truth. How I was unjustly thrown into the slammer. Locked up with the bad kids. She'll take my side—I'm her firstborn!

"School project," Lizzie blurted out. She swallowed hard, wondering where the lie had come from.

Mrs. McGuire raised one of her eyebrows. "School project?"

"It ran late," Lizzie lied again. She was kind of shocked—but she actually sounded convincing. "Sorry."

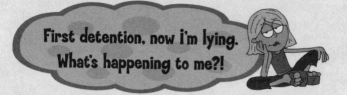

First detention, now i'm lying. What's happening to me?!

"Oh, it ran late," Mrs. McGuire said calmly. "Well, honey, why didn't you say so? Oh." She snapped her fingers. "I know why. Because you prefer to torture me! I mean, here I am, worried sick, imagining all sorts of terrible things!" Her voice rose until she was nearly shouting. "Lizzie, you know the rules. When you're late, you're supposed to call me!"

Lizzie sighed and nodded. "I get the point, Mom. I said I was sorry." She winked at her mother and added, "Don't stop the love."

Mrs. McGuire's face softened. But then she spun around and yelled, "Freeze!"

Lizzie turned to find her little brother, Matt, sneaking into the house, crawling on the floor, army style.

"But I didn't do it!" Matt yelled. Lizzie and her mother gave each other a baffled look, then stared at him.

Matt shrugged. "Reflex," he explained, then jumped to his feet and struck a casual pose. "So what's for dinner?"

"What's for dinner?" Mrs. McGuire shouted. "I'll tell you what's for dinner. Where have you been?"

Matt frowned thoughtfully. "Is that the other white meat?"

Mrs. McGuire was not amused. "Matt, you are supposed to be home when the streetlights come on, and the streetlights have been on for . . ." She glanced at the clock on the wall, which read 6:07—"exactly seven minutes." She turned to Lizzie. "Did you two plan this or something?"

Lizzie rolled her eyes. "Oh, yeah, like I'd plan anything with that double-E," she said.

Mrs. McGuire paused. She had absolutely no idea how to respond to that remark. So she turned back to Matt.

"I left early, Mom," Matt whined. "The game wasn't even finished yet. None of the other guys had to leave."

"Well, I don't care about the other guys," Mrs. McGuire said. "I care about you."

Nice try, Matt, Lizzie thought. Like that ever works. Like any parent anywhere falls for the "none of the other kids has to . . ." plea. Like mom was going to say, "Oh, okay! If none of the other kids has to come home, then you don't, either!" As if Lizzie hadn't tried that a dozen times before!

"But they all get to do stuff I don't!" Matt told her. "Like, go to scooter parks, and bungee jump—" Poor kid, Lizzie thought, he is definitely on the wrong train.

"Bungee jump?" Mrs. McGuire asked, aghast.

"They eat *all* their candy *on* Halloween," Matt continued. And *that* train is headed for Punishment Town! Lizzie thought.

Mrs. McGuire frowned. "That's their mothers' problem, not mine."

"And none of them have a bedtime!" Matt folded his arms and looked defiantly at his mother.

"None of those boys have a bedtime?" Matt's mother asked.

He just pulled into Grounded-ville, Lizzie thought. Now her mom will call one of these mothers, find out how so not true that is, and Matt will be banned from playtime again—ha-ha.

"Nope," said Matt.

Mrs. McGuire considered this for a moment. A sly look crossed her face. "Fine," she told Matt. "From now on, neither do you."

"What?" Matt's face lit up.

"What?!" Lizzie almost screamed. Lizzie and Matt stared at their mother.

"We'll make a deal," Mrs. McGuire said. "You come home when you're supposed to, and from now on, no bedtime."

"Mom, are you feeling okay?" Lizzie asked. Her mother nodded. Here's the plan, Lizzie thought: be nice to Matt for ten whole minutes, and then ask him to explain to me how he just did that.

Matt broke into a happy dance, holding his fingers above his head in a victory sign. "Whoo-hoo! Yeah! Touchdown!" he cried. He fully expected to lose valuable playtime, but instead he got—no bedtime. Was he good, or what?

Better plan, Lizzie thought: hang Matt up by his jacket and *make* him tell me how he just did that.

* * *

After dinner (which strangely enough *was* the other white meat, with a side of applesauce), Lizzie retreated to her bedroom for her nightly three-way call to Gordo and Miranda.

"So how was detention?" Gordo asked.

"Or do you need some time for the wounds to heal before you can talk about it?" Miranda said.

Lizzie couldn't wait to fill them in. "You guys won't believe it, but—"

"They let you out early for good behavior?" Gordo asked, cutting her off.

"They had you move to a separate room for your own protection?" Miranda guessed.

"No, listen!" said Lizzie. "It wasn't bad at all. In fact, it was kind of fun."

Seconds passed, and neither one said anything.

"This must be a bad connection, Gordo," Miranda said finally. "I think she just said that detention was fun."

"This is Lizzie, right?" Gordo asked. "Lizzie 'Good Girl' McGuire?"

"Hey, I'm not a good girl *all* the time, am I?" Lizzie asked, oddly insulted. "I mean, I've been bad on occasion, haven't I?"

"Um . . ." Gordo and Miranda said in unison. Lizzie lost sleep over the canned food drive, volunteered at the animal shelter, did charity walks for stuff she'd never even heard of, and never, ever forgot to recycle. *Of course* she was a good girl.

"Sorry, Lizzie," Gordo told her. "But you're kind of the good-girl prototype."

Lizzie groaned. "Do you know what that makes me?" she cried. "Boring! Boring, boring! Now, Angel—she's not boring at all. We were talking and—"

"Angel?" Miranda yelped, cutting Lizzie off again. "As in Angel Lieberman?"

"This connection's definitely bad," Gordo

said. "Sounds like you said you and Angel had an actual conversation One where she didn't have you pinned to the ground, dangling spit over your face."

"She plays by her own rules," Lizzie was happy to inform them. "It's exciting." Just then, they all heard a click on the line. "Hold on, you guys." Lizzie said. Someone in her house had picked up an extension, and they all knew who it was.

"I don't have a bedtime! I don't have a bed- time!" Matt sang into the phone.

Lizzie and her friends were used to the Matt phone tap. As always, the strategy was to wait silently until Matt got bored and hung up. But ten whole seconds passed. "I still don't have a bedtime!" Matt sang again.

"Matt! I'm gonna crush you!" Lizzie screamed. "You guys, I'll see you tomorrow," she said to her friends and clicked off. Then, cordless phone in hand, Lizzie charged down the hallway to pummel her little brother.

At lunch the next day, Miranda and Gordo were waiting for Lizzie in the cafeteria line. "Where is she?" Miranda asked, as she and Gordo finally carried their lunch trays loaded with mystery-meat chili to a nearby table. "She never misses lunch. It's her favorite class."

Just then, Lizzie and Angel pushed open the cafeteria doors, both laughing hysterically. Miranda and Gordo frowned. Lizzie looked different today. Instead of sporting her usual colorful digs, she was wearing a tight black shirt, old jeans, and a leather band around her blond ponytail. She almost looked like . . . Angel.

"The way you sneezed in front of Pettus, that was classic!" Angel howled as they approached the table where Miranda and Gordo were sitting.

"Well, the note I forged said I had a doctor's appointment, remember?" Lizzie replied. "I had to make it look realistic."

Miranda's and Gordo's mouths dropped open. "You forged a note?" Gordo cried.

Angel looked at him as if he was a squashed bug. "Get over it, Gor-dork," she said. "Frizz made it worth your while." Grinning, Lizzie pulled a slice of pizza from a paper bag and set it on the table.

Miranda gasped. Quickly, she grabbed a napkin and threw it over the slice.

"Hey, what are you doing?" Lizzie snapped, snatching the pizza back. "The cheese is going to get all gross."

Miranda stared at her friend in disbelief. "I'm hiding the evidence!" she said. "You obviously lost your mind and went off campus."

Angel sneered. "Can't get anything past you, can you, Sanchez?"

"Don't you have a car to steal or something?" Miranda replied sharply.

Angel made a threatening move toward Miranda, but Lizzie quickly stepped between them, saying, "Okay, come on, you guys." She turned to Miranda. "It's no B.D."

Miranda and Gordo looked at each other and raised their eyebrows. B.D.?

Lizzie rolled her eyes. "B.D.," she said slowly, like it was the most obvious thing in the universe. "Big deal."

Angel nudged Lizzie. "I'll catch you on the flip side, Frizz," she said. "Need to meet my tutor and go over my cheat sheet. And don't forget about Friday night."

"Coolie," Lizzie said. Lizzie and Angel slapped hands and wiggled their fingers at each other, then Angel headed out the door of the cafeteria. As soon as she was gone, Lizzie turned to her friends. "You really just ruined a perfectly good piece of pizza, Miranda," she said.

Miranda and Gordo stared at her.

"What?" Lizzie asked defensively.

"You must be suffering from post-traumatic detention syndrome," Gordo said, standing up to leave. "Why else would you be hanging out with Angel Lieberman? She's bad news, Lizzie."

Okay, so maybe Angel is a little dangerous. But a little danger never hurt a girl.

"You guys just don't know Angel the way I do," Lizzie told her friends as they exited the lunchroom.

"Yeah, and let's keep it that way," Miranda said.

"Okay, so maybe she is a little rough around the edges," Lizzie agreed. "But she knows about some really cool stuff—"

"Like parole?" Gordo suggested.

Lizzie frowned at him. "She has an answer for everything—"

"But she usually takes the fifth," Miranda interjected.

"And she's starting a band!" Lizzie exclaimed. "Nothing puts the double-O in cool like starting a band!"

Gordo and Miranda rolled their eyes. Lizzie ignored them. "Oh!" she said suddenly. "You guys should come to the party this weekend!"

"Oh, please, can we?" Gordo said sarcastically.

"It's a high-school party," Lizzie added.

"I'm going to a high-school party. Can you believe it?" She smiled at the horrified looks on Gordo's and Miranda's faces.

So long, good girl!
Hel-lo, Frizz!

"So," Lizzie said to her friends, "you guys in or what?"

CHAPTER THREE

That night, or rather, very very early the next morning, the McGuire house was dark and eerily quiet. The wall clock in the kitchen read 2:00 A.M. Everyone had long since gone to bed . . . everyone, that is, except Matt. Wearing a CD Walkman and his comfiest pajamas, Matt slid all the way across the living room floor in his sweat socks. Grabbing a tennis racket, he plucked at the strings like a crazed rock star. Then he jumped off the couch, and danced into the next toom. Matt had never felt so free. He had the whole house to himself, all the time in the world, and he was his own boss. This no-bedtime thing was *the coolest*.

Oh, Mama—but getting up the next morning was *the worst-est*. Slumped at the breakfast table, chin in hand, Matt could not keep his eyes open. He had two minutes until his toast would pop out of the toaster, so Matt decided to take a little nap. Standing nearby, well rested and drinking their morning coffee, his parents watched as drool ran down Matt's hand.

"Look at that poor kid," Mr. McGuire said to his wife. "He's not even going to make it to lunch."

"Trust me," Mrs. McGuire told him. "I know what I'm doing." She walked over to Matt and gently shook his shoulder. "Hey, sweetie," she said loudly. "How are you doing? How was your night last night?"

Matt startled awake and peered at her groggily. "Awesome night," he said.

"You know, I used to do some of my best thinking late at night," Mr. McGuire told him.

"I guess I thought about a few things," said Matt, wiping the mysterious drool off his chin. Oddly enough, he couldn't remember a single one of them.

"So how late do you think you stayed up?" Mr. McGuire asked.

"Late," Matt answered. "Real late."

Mr. and Mrs. McGuire looked at each other and raised their eyebrows. "That's impressive," Matt's mom said.

"Yeah," his dad agreed.

Matt felt a huge yawn coming on, but he didn't want to cop to it, so he moved the hand that was propping up his chin to cover his mouth. "I'm not even tired," he told his parents, casually strumming his fingers over his face.

"You *seem* tired," Mr. McGuire said.

Matt shook his head. "No, I'm just taking most . . . I mean, I'm just *making toast*!" he said quickly. Just as his toast popped out of the toaster, Lizzie strolled into the kitchen.

"I'll take that," she said, grabbing the toast.

"Lizzie, come on, that's your brother's breakfast—" Lizzie's mom started to scold, but suddenly something a lot more upsetting grabbed her attention. "What in heaven's name is in your nose?" she asked.

Lizzie's dad looked up and fumbled his coffee cup. Coffee spilled across the counter and dripped onto the floor, but Lizzie's parents didn't even notice. They were too busy staring at their sweet, innocent daughter. Or, more precisely, at the beaded ring in their sweet, innocent daughter's right nostril. Lizzie quickly held the piece of toast in front of her nose.

"Lizzie! What have you done to yourself?" Mr. McGuire asked, sounding almost frightened.

Lizzie held up her hands. "Take a chill pill, parents. It's just a temp."

Mrs. McGuire's mouth dropped open. "I don't even know where to start—your nose jewelry, your language, or your attitude," she said, her voice shaking.

"Let's start with her attitude," Matt offered happily. For *this* he was wide-awake.

"Matt! Eat your breakfast, please," his father commanded. Matt grabbed the toast from Lizzie's hand, and ducked out of the way before she could swat him.

"I'm sorry, Lizzie, but there is no way we're

letting you out of the house looking like that," Mr. McGuire said.

"But she looks this gross every day," Matt said from a safe distance.

Mrs. McGuire pointed a threatening finger at him. "Not a word," she warned.

Lizzie sighed and took the earring out of her nose. She held it up for her parents to see. "It's a fake, okay. I just wanted to see how it looked," she said with a sigh. "Relax."

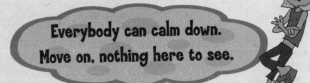

Everybody can calm down. Move on, nothing here to see.

Lizzie's mother shook her head in astonishment. "Honestly, I don't know what has gotten into you lately," she told Lizzie. But before she could even begin her rant, Mr. McGuire nudged her and pointed at Matt.

He was standing in the doorway of the kitchen, fast asleep, still holding the toast.

Lizzie looked at her parents. "And you think *I'm* the one with the problem?" she asked. She turned on her heel to walk out the door. "Sweet dreams," Lizzie said to her napping brother as she snatched the toast from Matt's hand when she passed him.

Instead of sweating it out in P.E. that day, Lizzie and Angel cut class and sneaked back into the girls' locker room. As they sat on a bench, doodling on their jeans, Lizzie smiled to herself. At that moment, the rest of their gymnauseous class was outside, running sprints. She had to admit it: being bad felt pretty good.

"That's it!" Angel said suddenly. She pointed to the electric guitar she'd just drawn on the knee of Lizzie's jeans. "That is exactly the tattoo I'm going to get."

Lizzie leaned over and examined the picture. "Before you start your band and L-squared, right?" she asked.

"Maybe that's what I should call my band," Angel said. "'L-Squared.'"

"Yeah." Lizzie nodded slowly. "It could catch on."

"By the way, cool jewels," Angel said, pointing at Lizzie's nose.

Lizzie touched the beaded hoop and grinned. She'd slipped the earring back onto her nose as soon as she had got to the school bus. "Thanks. My parents T.F.O.'d when they saw it," she told Angel.

Angel looked confused. Then she smiled. "T.F.O. Totally Freaked Out. Hey, good one. So," she said, leaning closer, "speaking of old folks, you know that party? No parents will be there. How sweet is that?"

Lizzie's smile froze.

No parents?

"There're also going to be boys there. Lots of them. Cute *high-school* boys," Angel told Lizzie. She grinned and raised her eyebrows. "Can you say Hottie High?"

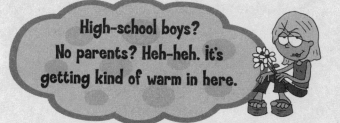

High-school boys? No parents? Heh-heh. it's getting kind of warm in here.

Angel looked carefully at her. "That's not a problem, is it, Frizz?" she asked.

Here it was. The moment of truth. Time to separate the girl with the curl from the Liz with the frizz. So why was Lizzie thinking about her mommy? Then again, Lizzie thought, flipping her reasoning, Matt broke the rules and he wound up without a bed-time. . . . "Uh, no," she said, shaking her head. "No problem at all."

Just then, Miranda entered the locker room, wearing her blue P.E. uniform and her hair in pigtails. When she spotted Lizzie sitting with Angel, her eyes narrowed.

"Hey, Miranda," Lizzie said coolly.

"Why aren't you in P.E.?" Miranda asked accusingly.

Lizzie shrugged. "Well, I thought about it. But then I was, like, what's the point? It's not like I plan on being a P.E. teacher when I grow up," she said. Angel snickered and held out her hand. Lizzie slapped it and wiggled her fingers.

Miranda stared at Lizzie, trying to find a glimpse of her old friend. She had to be in there somewhere beneath all that eyeliner, Miranda thought, but where? She wished she knew. But since she didn't, Miranda simply turned and stomped out the door. Lizzie and Angel watched her go and laughed.

After class, Miranda ran to Gordo's locker to share the latest on the Frizz front.

"Not only does Angel call her Frizz, which I totally don't get by the way, but she's ditching P.E., wearing a stupid hoop through her nose, and you know that party she invited us to? No adult supervision!" Miranda shook her head.

Gordo frowned. "I was hoping we wouldn't have to go there with her, but this is an emergency," he confided.

Miranda looked around, then whispered, "Go where? What are you talking about?"

"Scaring Lizzie straight," said Gordo. "She's a good girl at heart. We just need to remind her of that."

"And how are we going to do that?" Miranda asked.

But just as Gordo was about to explain his brilliantly devious scheme, Lizzie strode over with one of her own. "Okay, guys, Angel helped me work out a plan," she said. "Since you guys aren't going to the party Friday night, I'll say I'm sleeping over at your house, Miranda. If my parents call for any reason, you'll page me at the party to give me a heads up. Sam and Jo would freak if they knew where I really was." She shook her head at the thought, then lifted a hand. "Later," she said and walked away before either one could reply.

Gordo watched her leave, then turned to his locker and pulled out his video camera. "Intervention time," he said.

Miranda smiled. "Intervention?" she said. Of course! If it could get Gordo off his embarrassing obsession with the board game Dwarflord, why couldn't it get Lizzie off the Most Likely NOT to Succeed list?

CHAPTER FOUR

It was 11:34 P.M., and the McGuires' kitchen looked like a school cafeteria after a massive food fight. Candy wrappers, crushed potato chips, and peanut shells littered the kitchen counter. Squashed marshmallows were stuck to the floor in gooey gobs. But it hadn't taken an army of kids to do this damage. This was the aftermath of one kid's premidnight snack. And he wasn't finished yet. For dessert, Matt stood in front of the open refrigerator, drinking chocolate syrup straight out of the bottle.

Matt looked over at the wall clock and busted a grin. "The night is still young!" he cried, preparing for his after-hours party of one. Then he tipped his head back and squirted one more blast of syrup into his mouth.

By 12:02, Matt was parked in front of the television, ready for a night of cable TV. As he flipped through the channels, a commercial caught his attention. A man in a giant sequined turban stared out from the screen. In front of him, a crystal ball flickered.

"Now, knowing the future is just a phone call away," said the TV announcer. "Just dial 1-555-PREDICT and talk to one of our psychic pals. Just two dollars and ninety-five cents per minute. Call now. Offer void in Kansas, Alaska, and Hawaii."

What a coincidence! Matt had often

wondered what the future held for him. He put down the remote control, picked up the phone, and dialed 1-555-PREDICT.

One hour and twenty minutes later, Matt was still on the couch with the phone glued to his ear. "I'm going to be tall enough to play in the NBA?" he shouted into the receiver. "I'm going to be married how many times? I'm really going to be ruler of the free world? Oh, yeah!" He threw his fists in the air and bounced up and down on the couch, shouting, "Who's your ruler?"

The next morning, Mr. and Mrs. McGuire found Matt facedown in his bowl of cereal, sound asleep. As Mr. McGuire lifted his son's head and wiped off the flakes, Matt continued to snore. Even the sound of the ringing telephone didn't wake him up. Mr. McGuire laid Matt's face back into his cereal bowl and answered the phone.

"That was school," Mr. McGuire told his wife after he'd hung up the phone. "It seems they're concerned about Matt's home life. Seems Matt sneaked into the kindergarten room yesterday during nap time and slept through his next three classes."

"Well, at least he's sleeping somewhere," Mrs. McGuire said. She leaned over Matt's shoulder and shouted into his ear. "Morning, honey!"

"No more gravy!" Matt screamed, bolting straight up in his chair. He looked around the kitchen groggily. "Oh. It was just a dream," he said with a sigh. His chin sank back down onto his chest.

"So," Mrs. McGuire said loudly. "Are you still going to ride your scooter to school today?"

Matt yawned. "Okay," he said, without opening his eyes.

"Don't forget your helmet," Matt's dad added. He picked the bright blue helmet off the table and handed it to his son. Mrs. McGuire wheeled the scooter over to him.

"Here you go," Mrs. McGuire said. "Have fun."

"Fun," Matt mumbled. He stood up and picked up the helmet and a spoon. Placing the helmet sideways on his head, he shuffled toward the door like a sleepwalker, leaving his scooter behind. He opened the front door and left for school, wearing only his underwear, socks, and a T-shirt.

Mr. and Mrs. McGuire watched him go. "How far do you think he'll get before he realizes?" Mr. McGuire asked.

"Ahhhhhhhhh!" they heard Matt scream.

Mrs. McGuire smiled at her husband. "Not very far," she said.

That morning before homeroom, Miranda and Gordo stood in the hallway, waiting for

Lizzie. Miranda paced back and forth. She was totally nervous about their plan.

"You sure she's going to show?" Miranda asked Gordo.

He nodded. "I told her I had the answers to the algebra test. She'll show. Come on," he said, pointing to a nearby classroom. "Before she sees you."

Miranda ducked inside. A second later, Lizzie came down the hall. She was wearing a studded leather vest she had borrowed from Angel over a black mesh T-shirt and jeans with large rips at the knees. Her blond hair was teased into a spiky ponytail, and she had another hoop earring clamped to her nose. Now she looked more like Angel than . . . Angel.

Lizzie walked up to Gordo and glanced around furtively like a practiced criminal. "You got the goods?" she asked in a low voice.

"In here," Gordo said, nodding at the nearby classroom.

"Well?" Lizzie said impatiently once they were inside. She blinked as her eyes adjusted to the darkened room. Suddenly, Miranda stood up and popped a videotape into the classroom's VCR.

"Miranda?" Lizzie said, surprised. Gordo grabbed her arm and pulled her into one of the nearby desk seats. Miranda came and stood on her other side. Lizzie was trapped.

"Hey, what's going on?" Lizzie cried.

"It's called an intervention. We want you back," Miranda stated plainly.

"I haven't gone anywhere," Lizzie said, annoyed.

"That's what you think," said Gordo. He aimed the remote control and pushed "Play." A photo of Lizzie wearing a black tie-dyed T-shirt, spiky pigtails, and the nose ring came onto the screen. Lizzie recognized the outfit she'd worn to school the day before, but she was having a harder time recognizing herself.

"This week, on Before They Were Bad Girls, *The Lizzie McGuire Story*," Gordo's voice said on the video.

The image changed to a cutesy picture of Lizzie as a baby. "Lizzie McGuire started out life as a good girl. She had it all: friends, family, and three-way calling," Gordo said in the voice-over. Like a news-magazine show, the video flashed through a series of photos: Lizzie in second grade; Lizzie with her parents and Matt on Christmas morning; Lizzie, Miranda, and Gordo all chatting on the phone.

Just then the image switched to a close-up of Miranda. In a blond wig and glasses with square frames, she almost looked like Mrs. McGuire. On the screen below her, it read LIZZIE'S MOM.

"Lizzie was such a good baby," Miranda-as-Mrs. McGuire said to the camera. "The way she napped. And not once, not once, did she ever eat dirt."

Lizzie crossed her arms over her chest, sat back, and glanced over at Miranda. This was definitely weird.

Suddenly, the camera changed angles, and Gordo's face filled the screen. He was dressed to look like Lizzie's dad in wire-rimmed glasses and a red button-down shirt. His hair was slicked back with too much gel. At the bottom of the screen, written on a card, were the words LIZZIE'S DAD.

"Yeah. She always ate her vegetables and finished her milk," said Gordo-as-Mr. McGuire. "She laughed a lot. So good-natured. She was a good kid."

"This is ridiculous," Lizzie said. She stood up to bolt, but Miranda placed a hand on her shoulder and pushed her back down into her seat.

"It's for your own good, Lizzie," she said.

Different shots of Hillridge Junior High School appeared on the TV screen. "Fast-forward to junior high, where Lizzie went from good baby to good girl," explained Gordo's voice-over.

The image changed to Miranda being interviewed in the school hallway. "We were best friends," Miranda told the camera. "We ate lunch together every day. Had slumber parties. I still have the friendship bracelet she gave me on the first day of junior high."

The interview with Miranda cut to grainy, black-and-white footage of Angel walking down the hallway. "But the good days came crashing down when she met a devil named Angel," Gordo's voice-over explained. On the screen, Angel made a face at the camera.

"Everything was fine until Lizzie got detention," Gordo went on. The video cut to a shot of the detention room door, followed by an interview with the drama teacher who ran detention.

"Lizzie McGuire?" the teacher asked the camera. His brow wrinkled as he tried to remember. "What exactly was she in for?" He reached over his shoulder, discovering yet another note taped to his back.

"She was in for cheating at math," Gordo said in the voice-over, "but soon she'd be cheating at life."

The image cut to the McGuire living room. Matt was fast asleep in a chair. Miranda crouched behind the chair, moving his arms like a puppet and talking for him. "She used to live up there," said Miranda-as-Matt as she pointed Matt's arm toward Lizzie's bedroom. "Now she lives out on the street. The horror!"

Miranda dramatically covered Matt's face with his hands.

The image switched to another shot of Miranda, now dressed like bad girl McGuire in a torn T-shirt, spiky blond wig, and a nose ring. "Lizzie planned on going to parties she was too young for. Put earrings in places they're not meant to be." The camera zoomed in on Miranda's nose ring. "Forgery, ditching, and lying became a way of life. Lizzie got too fast even for the fast crowd." With each bad deed, the images of Miranda became tougher and tougher until, in the last shot, she was covered in fake tats and phony piercings.

"If we don't stop her now, she could end up in jail. Or worse!" Miranda's voice cried from the TV as the video showed the real Lizzie walking down the school hallway in slow motion.

Gordo appeared on-screen, looking like himself. "Which is why we made this film,"

Gordo said to the camera. Miranda came and stood next to him.

"For you, Lizzie McGuire," they said together.

The film ended. Lizzie stared at the blank screen, stunned. Then she stood up and addressed her friends. "I can't believe you took the time to make such a . . . bad movie," she told them.

Miranda looked at Gordo. "I thought you said this would work!" she cried.

"I do have to say," Lizzie added, softening a bit, "I think it's pretty cool that you guys care so much about me. And you did go to all that trouble. But I have to ask . . ." She pointed at the TV screen. "Does my hair always look that bad?"

Gordo stared at her. "You mean to tell me that you're actually okay with ditching and all that other stuff?" he asked, dismayed.

Lizzie thought back to all the lies she'd told

and the sneaking around she'd done in just the past few days. "Actually, no. I mean, being a bad girl all the time is hard work." She shrugged her shoulders and grinned. "Guess I really am just a good girl at heart." Besides, Lizzie thought, she looked so much nicer when she was nice.

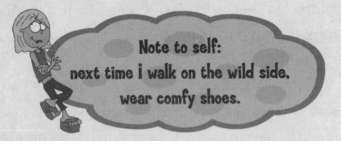

Note to self:
next time i walk on the wild side,
wear comfy shoes.

Gordo and Miranda smiled back at her. "So, next Friday. The usual?" asked Gordo.

"Popcorn and a rental at my house?" Miranda said.

"Sounds G.T.M.—ooh!" Lizzie scrunched up her face, catching herself. "Never mind," she said. "Sounds good to me." Actually, she thought, she *would* miss the shorthand lingo.

CHAPTER FIVE

Later that day, minus the nose ring and tattered clothes, Lizzie was on her way to good old Mrs. Wortman's math class when Angel stopped her in the hall. "Hey, Frizz," Angel said. "Did you get the answers for the test from Gor-dork?"

"Okay." Lizzie leveled Angel with a cool stare. "A, my name is Lizzie, not Frizz. B, Gordo's no dork—he's one of my best friends. And C, I don't cheat."

Angel blinked in surprise. Then she curled her lip, quickly becoming menacing Angel again. "Fine," she snapped. "But if you think you're going to be in my band now, you're *so* not. And you, Lizzie McGuire, are never going to L-squared."

"Ooooh." Lizzie moaned sarcastically, then added, "I think I'll live."

As Angel stomped off, Lizzie smiled to herself. Living large had a totally different meaning to her now. It was more like taking all the small stuff like great friends and cool parents and seeing how much it added up to. Which was *a lot*.

That night, after Lizzie finished her homework, she went to the kitchen to get something to drink. She found Matt sitting at the counter, eating from a bag of potato chips.

"Staying up late again?" Lizzie asked as she grabbed a can of soda from the refrigerator.

"No way," Matt told her. "I'm exhausted. I asked Mom and Dad to give me back my bedtime."

Lizzie joined her brother at the counter and took a few chips from the bag. "It's funny," she said, smiling. "In a way, I just got my bedtime back, too."

Matt looked at her. "You are really dumb," he said.

"No," Lizzie replied. "But sometimes it may seem that way."

Matt shook his head. "No. You really are."

Lizzie frowned at him. Then she snatched the bag of chips and held them out of his reach.

"Hey!" Matt cried. "I was there first." He lunged around her and grabbed the other side of the bag.

"Too bad, I'm bigger," said Lizzie.

"Too bad, I'm faster," said Matt, taking off with the bag. Lizzie chased him around the kitchen. Even a good girl has her limits!

PART TWO

CHAPTER ONE

"**W**here's Gordo?" Miranda asked Lizzie as they hit the schoolyard for lunch. "I thought we were supposed to meet him."

It was a typical spring day at Hillridge Junior High. All around, kids were lounging on benches and tables, listening to the same short list of radio-overplayed straight pop, hip-hop, and punk-pop songs on their boom boxes.

But on this day something swinging suddenly jumped into the music mix. And that's when Lizzie knew exactly where Gordo was to be found. "Just follow the music. And get ready to travel back in time," Lizzie said, rolling her eyes.

They rounded the corner, and there he was. Alone on a picnic table, leaning back on one elbow, snapping his fingers along to the steady beat of the big band number bouncing out of his portable stereo. And as if that wasn't dorky enough, there was the matter of what he was wearing—namely, a checkered fedora with a pink-and-orange-paisley hat-band and a vintage bowling shirt with some-one else's name on it.

"Hey, Gordo," Lizzie said, glancing around.

Gordo looked up at them. "Hey, pally. Charlie, how's your bird?"

Lizzie and Miranda looked at each other and raised their eyebrows. Their "bird"?

"I just said, 'Hey, how's it going?' That's

how they talked in Las Vegas in 1960," Gordo explained.

Miranda visibly cringed. "Can't you just talk normal?" she begged. "Like, 'Hey Dog, what's the dilly-o?'"

Gordo shook his head. "That's how everybody talks," he replied. "I'm not everybody."

Lizzie smiled at this understatement of the century. Gordo was *definitely* not everybody. He was always doing something different. When everybody else at school was Rollerblading, Gordo was riding a unicycle. And when everybody was into chocolate cappuccino, Gordo was drinking some weird plum soda. His latest obsession was Rat Pack lounge culture. Lately, he was spending all of his free time buying old record albums with titles like *Songs for Swingin'* and *In the Wee Small Hours.* And all his clothes looked like he'd raided his grandfather's closet.

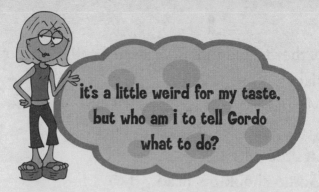

it's a little weird for my taste, but who am i to tell Gordo what to do?

But after the fifth weird look from *everybody else*, Lizzie decided she was Gordo's best friend, that's who. "Gordo, shouldn't you be listening to Britney Spears?" she said, hoping to nudge him into acceptance-ville.

Gordo looked blank. "Why?" he asked.

"Because that's what normal people do," Miranda informed him.

Lizzie agreed. "We don't want people thinking that you're weird," she said.

Gordo leaned over and handed Lizzie a folded twenty-dollar bill. "Do me a solid, doll. Take this double sawbuck and grab me a platter I got on tap."

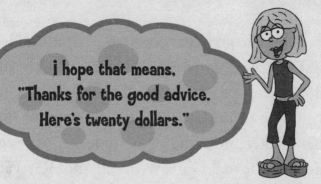

i hope that means,
"Thanks for the good advice.
Here's twenty dollars."

"The new Rat Pack CD compilation is in at Getta Load A' Disc," Gordo said, naming their favorite indie music store. "It's totally remastered—and I was sorta hoping you could pick it up for me after school."

"Why can't *you* pick it up?" Lizzie asked. "Are you headlining in Atlantic City?" Miranda giggled and helped herself to some of Gordo's corn chips.

"I've got something on my toe," Gordo admitted.

What does that "something on my toe" mean in Rat-Pack-speak, Lizzie wondered. Does he have to run?

"I have to go to the podiatrist," Gordo added.

Ew! Lizzie groaned. Miranda quickly put down the chips. "Okay, I'll pick it up for you," Lizzie said, tucking Gordo's money into her pocket and standing up to leave. "But you do *me* a favor. Go easy on all this Rat Pack stuff, okay?"

"Go *easy*?" Gordo cried. "How can you go easy with a rompin' cat like Frank?" Lizzie and Miranda rolled their eyes and headed back into school. "You gotta hear him *swing*, baby!" Gordo called after them. "He could make 'Old MacDonald' jump." Turning up the volume on his box, Gordo began to sing along with the music. "Old MacDonald had a farm, E-I-E-I-O."

Suddenly, a half-eaten peanut-butter sandwich flew through the air and whacked him in the head. "Stop playing that junk!" a kid yelled. "You're ruining my lunch!"

Gordo reached over and turned down the volume. "Maybe I *could* tone it down a little," he admitted to no one in particular.

The next morning, Miranda climbed aboard the school bus and made her way to the seat Lizzie had saved for her. "Hey, did you get Gordo's CD?" she asked.

Lizzie pulled the disc from her backpack and held it out as if—at any moment—it could emit a foul odor. On the cover, a group of men with colorful shirts and slicked-back hair was clustered around an old-fashioned microphone. "I told the clerk it's for my great-grandfather who's too frail to leave the Home," she told Miranda.

Just then, a freckled hand reached over her shoulder and snatched the CD away from her. Lizzie and Miranda twisted around in their seats. Vince, an annoying kid with curly red hair who lived to make yellow bus travel as loathsome as possible, waved the CD at them.

"Vince, give it!" Miranda demanded. She tried to grab the CD, but he yanked it out of her reach.

"'Ooh, I'm Miranda. I want my CD back!'" Vince said in a fake girly voice.

Lizzie held out her open hand. "Seriously, Vince, it's not for us. It's for somebody else."

"'Seriously, I'm Lizzie. I borrowed someone's CD!'" Vince said in a phony, high-pitched voice that he somehow thought sounded like Lizzie's.

"She didn't borrow it," Miranda snapped. "She got it for Gordo."

Vince's eyes lit up. "'Ooh, I'm Lizzie. I'm in l-o-o-o-ve with Gordo!'" he squealed, doing the worst Lizzie impression ever.

Suddenly, Ethan Craft reached across the aisle, grabbed Vince's wrist, and pulled him in. "Yo, Vince," he said, all up in Vince's face. "Give it up."

"Yeah, okay," Vince whimpered, releasing his grip. Ethan plucked the CD out of Vince's hand and smiled. Lizzie stared at Ethan. His wavy blond hair flopped over his forehead, and he was wearing a bright blue T-shirt that perfectly matched his eyes. Not to mention the fact that he had just saved her life. Okay, so he had just saved Gordo's eleven-dollar CD. Same diff. One thing she knew for certain:

Ethan Craft is so totally hot.

Ethan studied the Rat Pack CD. "This yours?" he asked Lizzie.

Lizzie's heart started to pound, and suddenly she could feel her cheeks growing pink.

"Thanks," she said, and hoping to get past the embarrassing music subject, she added, "Vince is a foot fungus."

"Fungus." Ethan agreed, glancing at Vince who was now quietly studying his shoes. Ethan flipped the CD over and took a look. "Isn't this, like, a million years old?"

Lizzie winced.

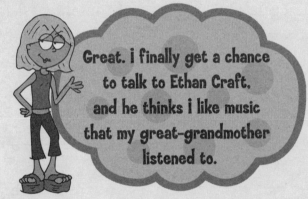

Great. i finally get a chance to talk to Ethan Craft, and he thinks i like music that my great-grandmother listened to.

"Mind if I check it out?" Ethan asked. Without waiting for an answer, he slipped the CD into his boom box. Frank Sinatra's crooning voice began to ooze out from the speakers.

Miranda and Lizzie slipped down in their seats, dreading what was to come.

"You don't understand, Ethan," Miranda began.

"We really don't listen to that kind of music. . . ." Lizzie turned to explain, but Ethan's head was actually bobbing along to the music.

"Hey, this kinda rocks," he said.

Lizzie and Miranda were completely floored. Ethan *liked* Gordo's music? Yo! What was going on here?

"Because it's not really the swingin'-est cut on the platter," Lizzie said quickly, changing her tune.

Miranda nodded. "Yeah, but with a rompin' cat like this guy, all the tunes are . . . are . . ." She searched her memory, trying to think what Gordo would say. "Are *groovin' birds*!" she finished. Lizzie and Miranda grinned at Ethan. They had no idea what they'd just said, but it sounded good.

Ethan turned up the volume. "This is old school," he said. "You guys have cool taste."

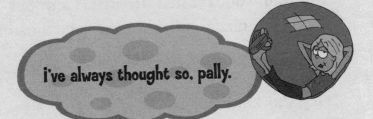

"Maybe we could hook up later—you know, hang out," Ethan said, handing the CD back to Lizzie. "You guys could give me the 4-1-1."

Lizzie's heart skipped a beat. Ethan Craft wanted to hang out with her? "Sure," she said, hoping she sounded casual. "We're experts." Okay, so that wasn't totally true, but she figured they could *become* experts. Like, really fast.

Miranda and Lizzie turned back around in their seats and smiled at each other. Gordo had totally hit on something with this whole Rat Pack thing. Maybe, Lizzie thought, he was right about unicycles, and plum soda, too! Maybe, Lizzie thought, she should ask Ethan to go unicycling after school, and then they could share a plum soda float . . . then again, she thought, maybe not. Still, the swing music thing was dead-on. Lizzie peeked over her shoulder at Ethan, and in a flash she imagined him dipping her in a serious swing dip . . . or whatever it was called!

CHAPTER TWO

Minutes before first period, Lizzie and Miranda were at their lockers, stashing their books when Gordo finally showed. "Hi, guys," he said.

Lizzie turned around. "Hey, how's your corn pone, baby?" she said cheerfully.

Gordo's eyebrows lifted in surprise. "Wow, where'd you learn that?" he asked, impressed.

Miranda showed Gordo the Rat Pack CD. "We read the back of this album," she told him. "This Sinatra cat was one mothery gasser."

Gordo eyed them suspiciously. "You guys aren't ragging on me, are you?"

"No, we really listened to this stuff," Lizzie assured him. "It grows on you."

"Trust me, Gordo," Miranda clarified. "If we wanted to rag on you, there'd be other ways to do it. For instance, you always watch movies with subtitles. . . ."

Gordo filtered out the subtitle slam and focused on the compliment. "Well, I'm glad you guys finally gave this stuff a chance," he said, walking toward his locker. Lizzie and Miranda followed him.

"Actually," Lizzie said to Gordo as he dialed his locker combination. "I was hoping you could teach me more about this stuff."

"Your middle name is Zephyr," Miranda went on, still listing ways they could rag on

Gordo, if they really wanted to. "What's *that* about?"

Gordo ignored the middle-name slam, too. "Sure, I can teach you," he told Lizzie. "Rat Pack, Louis Prima, Nat King Cole, how to talk, how to dress. I can get you all locked up, Charley Bangs." He shut his locker and smiled to himself. Finally, Gordo thought, his friends were trying to appreciate his unique taste.

"And there's that way you blink your eyes so much," Miranda yelled out, just now remembering the most rag-able Gordo quality yet.

This slam Gordo could not ignore. "I do not blink that much," he snapped.

"You *always* blink," said Miranda.

"I do not," Gordo said, blinking.

"You just did it," said Miranda, pointing at his face. Gordo blinked. "You did it again!" she cried.

"That's 'cause you're making me think about it," Gordo said, flustered. He blinked rapidly three times in a row.

"You did it again," said Miranda.

"Cut it out!" Gordo cried. Miranda looked shocked. She was just listing things they *could* rag on him for—it wasn't like she was *actually* ragging on him. Couldn't he see the difference? Gordo blinked. Miranda smiled. Gordo scowled. Then, they both stormed off in opposite directions. Lizzie didn't even notice. Swing music played in her head as she walked to class. She was just finishing that imaginary dance with Ethan. . . .

After school that afternoon, Matt and his best pal, Lanny, were playing an intense game of Net Ball in the McGuires' backyard. As they rallied, Matt counted off.

"Twenty-seven, twenty-eight, twenty-nine,

thirty . . ." Matt flung the ball to Lanny, who reached his net out for it, and then somehow totally missed it. Surprised, they watched the ball drop to the ground and roll under a shrub.

"We're getting better," Matt said, fetching the ball. "Ready to go again, Lanny?"

Lanny indicated that he was indeed still holding his net. That was pretty much all one had to do to be ready for Net Ball.

But before Matt could serve, his parents came into the yard carrying a tray of pansies, a bag of fertilizer, and some gardening tools.

"Hey, Matt. Hiya, Lanny!" Mr. McGuire called.

Lanny turned and looked at him.

"What are you boys up to?" Mrs. McGuire asked.

"We're gonna set the world record for the world's longest Net Ball rally, and then our world record will go in the book of world records," Matt told them excitedly.

"That's great," Mr. McGuire said. He turned to Lanny. "You think you got enough energy for that?"

Lanny just stared at him.

"Does he ever say anything?" Mr. McGuire whispered to his wife.

Mrs. McGuire shrugged. "I've never heard him speak," she whispered back.

"That's creepy," Mr. McGuire said.

"Maybe he's just shy," Mrs. McGuire replied in a hopeful tone. "Okay," she said to the boys. "You guys have fun." She turned to Lanny. "And you let us know if you need anything, okay?"

Lanny said nothing.

"Ready to go again, Lanny?" Matt asked. He served him the ball. "One . . ."

Trying to show their support, Matt's

parents watched for a moment. After all, their only son was practicing for global Net Ball immortality. But after two rallies died with scores under five, the McGuire parents shrugged and headed for the garden.

The next day in the school cafeteria, Lizzie and Miranda were waiting for a scoop of green gelatinous fruit mold (other option: gray meat and noodle soup) when Gordo caught up with them. Looking them over, he whistled. "Hey, check you guys out. You look like you just flew in from Acapulco."

Lizzie and Miranda turned and posed to fully show off their 1960s retro outfits. Lizzie had on a daisy-print minidress with a yellow chiffon scarf tied around her neck. Miranda was wearing a geometric-print sundress and a chunky wooden necklace.

"Crazy rags, huh?" Miranda said. She

poked at a plastic-wrapped sandwich, and then, deciding to operate on faith, placed it on her lunch tray.

As Lizzie slid her tray along the lunch counter, a boy from her algebra class waved at her. "Hey, Adam. How's your corn pone?" Lizzie called back. Confused, the boy lifted his arm and sniffed his armpit.

Gordo looked at Lizzie, concerned. "Um, guys, it's really cool that you're so into this," he said. "But please don't make too big a deal of it. I don't want it to turn into some dopey fad that every idiot starts doing just because he thinks it's trendy. Like Ricky Martin. And Digital Pets."

"Digital Pets were fun," Miranda said, instantly lost in the memory. "I was so sad when mine died." Gordo stared at her. *This* from the girl who made fun of him for watching movies with subtitles.

Lizzie sniffed her food, but it still remained a mystery. "Don't worry, Gordo," she said. "It's not like we're the trendsetters around here."

Just then, Ethan Craft sauntered over. He was wearing a red sweater that showed off his tan, and his wavy hair was perfectly slicked back. To Lizzie, he looked like a Greek god. Better than a Greek god, Lizzie thought, remembering a statue she had once seen. Wreaths and togas were simply not a good look. No comeback on the wreath and toga fad, Lizzie privately wished to herself.

"Hey, Lizzie, Miranda." Ethan smiled at them with his perfect white teeth, then turned to Gordo. "Yo, Gor-*don*," he said. Gordo scowled.

"I was just noticing your shirt," Ethan said, pointing to the blue polyester bowling shirt Gordo was wearing. "Very Mack Daddy."

"Uh, thanks," Gordo said.

"Where'd you get it?" Ethan asked.

"Actually, it was a gift from my aunt," Gordo lied. "She lives in Rangoon, and they're all out of this kind of shirt." He moved his tray down the counter, trying to edge away from Ethan.

"Bummer, man," Ethan said. "Cool shirt, though."

"Ethan, Miranda and I got *these* clothes at Anteater over on Lexington Street," Lizzie gladly offered. Gordo glared at her, but Lizzie didn't even notice. She was having a moment with Ethan. "They had a lot of guy-stuff, too," she added.

"And they accept all major credit cards." Miranda jumped in, not wanting to miss her chance to talk to Ethan . . . even if it was about point-of-sale options.

"Cool. I'm there. Props, man," Ethan said

by way of thanks. He turned and sauntered over to a group of kids hanging out near the door. "Come on, Steve," Gordo heard him say. "We're going to Anteater."

Gordo watched uneasily as Ethan and his friend took off to raid his favorite store.

CHAPTER THREE

"Thiry-five . . . thirty-six . . ." Matt was counting. His voice rising in excitement with each higher number, his dream of Net Ball greatness getting closer and closer with each return . . . Until, suddenly, the ball dropped to the ground at Matt's feet. Matt and Lanny stared at it. "Ugh—thirty-five." Matt threw down his Net Ball racket, and then threw himself down after it. There was only one thing left for Matt to do. Have a major temper tantrum. "Crud!" he yelled. "That's the best we've done in two days. This is pointless."

Matt and Lanny flopped down on the patio chairs. Matt put his chin in his hands and looked unhappily at the book of world records that was sitting on the table. It seemed like they'd never beat the all-time, worldwide, Net Ball championship record now. Which meant they'd never get their names into that stupid book.

Unless . . . Lanny turned to Matt and raised his eyebrows.

"Hey, that's a great idea!" Matt said. "We can find a *different* record to set!" Matt grabbed the world record book from the patio table and began to thumb through it. "Let's see," he said. "World's Land Speed Record? Nah." He shook his head. "We can't drive. World's Tallest Man? Nah . . . Here we go—World's Largest Pancake!" He and Lanny looked at each other. No words were necessary.

In the McGuires' kitchen, Matt and Lanny grabbed a bag of flour and dumped it into the biggest salad bowl they could find. They added a gallon of milk, half a carton of eggs, and the rest of a can of baking powder. Matt tossed Lanny a big spoon and took turns stirring. Soon they were both covered in batter.

As Matt heated a giant skillet on the stove, Lanny unwrapped a stick of butter and threw it in the pan. Together they lifted the huge slopping salad bowl over to the stove. As they poured out the thick batter, they dreamed the dreams of breakfast champions.

Minutes later, the pancake started bubbling. But there was a pothole in the road to greatness. How were they going to flip it? Armed with two spatulas, a wooden spoon, and salad tongs, they attacked it from both sides, but they were no match for the doughy monster. It wouldn't flip, so it started to burn. Matt turned off the stove. The boys stared at the charred and gooey mess. Their enormous pancake dream was now but a fading memory.

"Let's find something else to do," Matt said at last. Lanny nodded. Together they carried the enormous skillet over to the sink. But when they turned on the water, the overheated pan started to smoke. Matt watched it with alarm and turned to Lanny. "Don't tell my mom about this," he said pleadingly. Lanny nodded: mum's the word.

Upstairs, Lizzie and Miranda were hard at work on a seemingly impossible feat of their own. They had spent days mixing and matching dresses, hats, shoes, bags, jewelry—each trying to perfect her own unique retro look.

After some serious misses (no white tights for Lizzie, definitely no beehives for Miranda), it finally paid off. By the following Monday they could only look at each other and think, What a tomato! Sporting teal Capri pants, a paisley-print sleeveless sweater, and green chiffon scarf, Lizzie was one motherly beetle. And in her bright orange minidress, Miranda was definitely a ring-a-ding doll.

That is, they looked pretty cool.

"There was a Frank Sinatra biography on TV last night," Gordo said, as he, Lizzie, and Miranda walked to their lockers after Mrs. Wortman's math class. "Did you know that he spent more money on hats than my house cost. . . ?" Gordo broke off suddenly, gaping at the scene before him. The hallway was filled with boys in straw fedoras and bowling shirts and girls in brightly colored minidresses. They all looked like they had stepped straight off Gordo's Rat Pack album cover.

Lizzie looked around and smiled. You gotta hand it to the kids at our school, she thought. They sure can jump on a moving bandwagon. And fast.

It's a good thing Gordo's CD wasn't banjo music. Everybody would be dressed like hillbillies.

"This is so great, Gordo. Everybody loves your music!" Lizzie beamed at Gordo. But he seemed less than flattered.

Just then, Miranda spotted Kate making a beeline toward them through the hallway. "Kate alert. Kate alert," Miranda said through clenched teeth.

Lizzie's smile faded. Kate Sanders had been Lizzie's best friend in grade school until she totally transformed into a too-cool-for-Lizzie, popular cheerleader. They called her the Queen of the Killer She-Bees because there was always a swarm of similar-looking girls around her. And whenever Kate Sanders had something to say to Lizzie or her friends, it usually stung.

"Lizzie! Miranda!" Kate said, smiling as if they were her two favorite people in the world. Weirder still, she was all alone.

"Kate," Lizzie said guardedly.

"People are talking about you two," Kate told them.

"Yeah, well it's all lies!" Miranda blurted out.

Kate looked at her, confused. "They're saying that you guys started all this cool lounge stuff," she said. "That you were the *first ones*."

"Oh." Miranda nodded. "Yeah, that was us."

"Actually, it was Gordo who started it," Lizzie admitted. "But we ran with it."

"Well, whoever started it, you three were ahead of the curve," Kate said. "Which means . . . I need your help."

Well, well, well. Little Miss Popular needs our help. Looks like the shoe's on the other foot. But she's gonna have to beg. She's gonna have to get down on her knees. She's gonna have to *grovel*.

"Sure, Kate," Lizzie said cheerfully. "What do you need?"

Duh!

Note to self, Lizzie thought—look up the word *grovel*.

"I'm on the dance committee, and we thought it would be fun to give this month's party a Rat Pack theme. You guys . . ." Kate hesitated. Gordo looked at her, horrified. Lizzie and Miranda held their breath. ". . . can help us plan it," Kate finished reluctantly.

Lizzie tried to hide her excitement. She shrugged, "I think we could, because—"

"We can probably manage to—" Miranda jumped in.

"Because I don't think we have any other—"

"I've got some free time—"

"Yeah, we can do it," Lizzie and Miranda said in unison.

"Great." Kate smiled. "It should be a ding-dong time."

Gordo slammed his locker shut and turned

to Kate. "The phrase is 'ring-a-ding-ding,'" he growled.

"Whatever," Kate said. "It'll be fun." With a flip of her long blond hair, she strode away.

"Oh, Gordo, we can use those great Las Vegas posters that you got!" Lizzie squealed. "Oh, this is gonna be awesome." Miranda nodded happily.

"No, thanks," Gordo replied. "If you ask me, the idea of a Rat Pack dance couldn't be any stupider." He picked up his books. "See ya around, pally," he said, sounding somewhat less than pally, and headed off to class without them.

CHAPTER FOUR

That afternoon, Lizzie went over to Gordo's house for their usual study session. But when she tapped on his bedroom door, he didn't answer. Lizzie waited, then pushed the door open. Gordo was sitting alone in his room, painting a model airplane. Lizzie smiled and held up two chocolate cupcakes.

"Hey, Gordo, your mom sent up some cupcakes," she said. She took a bite of one and set the other on his desk.

"No, thanks," Gordo said without looking at her. He stood up and placed the airplane on a shelf next to another model plane. "One of her patients baked those. She lives in a one-bedroom apartment with twenty-eight cats."

"Ew." Lizzie dropped the rest of her cupcake into the trash can.

Just what i need. A hair ball.

"Anyway, I hope *you* understand this geography homework," Lizzie said cheerfully. "'Cause I don't see what job I could ever have that would possibly require me to know about Bolivia."

Gordo looked at her. "Ambassador to Bolivia," he said flatly.

"Oh," Lizzie said. Gordo turned back to his planes. "Whoa, aren't those the planes that your aunt gave you for your birthday?" Lizzie asked. "I thought you thought they were goofy."

"That's what I *thought*," Gordo replied. "They're actually kind of cool. The Allies used this plane in World War II to deliver powdered eggs and rubber to American Samoa." He held up the yellow plane for Lizzie to see.

"Wow, that's so cool," Lizzie said, trying to sound interested. She paused for a moment, then added, "Anyway, Gordo, everyone's really excited about this whole Rat Pack dance."

Gordo snorted.

"Oh, come on," Lizzie said. "I know you don't like dancing, but it could still be fun."

"It's not the dancing," Gordo told her. "I'm just not into that Rat Pack thing anymore."

Not into it? That's nuts!

"Oh, come on. You love it," Lizzie wheedled.

But Gordo shook his head. "Not anymore. Now I love radio-controlled, one-sixty-fourth-scale World War II planes. Vroom." He set the plane back on the shelf.

"How could you just give that up?" Lizzie asked.

"Fine," Gordo snapped. "I'll tell you why. It's because you and Miranda got Ethan Craft into it, and then he got everybody else into it. When Kate Sanders likes something, it's officially a Mindless Fad and I don't want any part of it."

"Gordo, I think Kate might really like it," Lizzie said.

"She thinks it's 'ding-dong!'" Gordo shouted, throwing his hands in the air with exasperation. "The phrase is 'ring-a-ding-ding!' It was a code for living life on your own terms. A Ding Dong is a chocolate-covered devil's food treat intended for mass consumption. *I'm not into mass consumption.*" He picked up his geography book and banged it down on the desk. "Let's do homework."

Lizzie's face fell. She'd had no idea Gordo was so upset. Or maybe she just wasn't paying attention because of all the extra Ethan attention she'd been basking in. . . .

Great. I've ruined Gordo's hobby, and I ate a cat-hair cupcake.

Meanwhile, over at Lizzie's house, two more kids were exploring a totally different form of *mass consumption*. In fact, they were hoping to set a world record in it.

Stuffing potato chips into his mouth, Lanny stood on the bathroom scale, while Matt monitored his pal's weight gain.

Suddenly, Matt thought he saw the needle on the scale move. "You've gained a pound!" he cried. "You have six hundred and seventy-four to go." Lanny nodded and crammed more chips into his mouth.

"Faster!" Matt shouted, cheering him on.

But when they realized how long it would actually take for Lanny to outgain the heaviest man in the world, they skipped to the Most Consecutive Jumps with a Jump Rope record. When they tripped up on that one (ouch!), they tried for the coveted Highest Tower of Cups and Saucers Balanced on a

Person's Head record. This one was totally happening. Matt was about to add the eighth cup and saucer to the stack on Lanny's head, when Mr. and Mrs. McGuire walked into the kitchen, carrying bags of groceries. Too bad Mrs. McGuire said something about its being her "best china," because that just made Matt and Lanny nervous, which caused the stack to wobble and then *crash!*

Next up was the Longest Sustained Singing Note. Lanny grabbed the stopwatch as Matt warmed up. Then Matt, posing like an opera singer, belted out his chosen note. It was a horrible off-key note, but Matt was committed and he wouldn't let it go. He kept pushing it out of his lungs until he completely ran out of air and collapsed on the floor. Lanny shook his head. Only twenty-five seconds. Not quite good enough.

It was almost dark by the time they

decided to set the world record for Running Up and Down a Flight of Stairs. Matt stood at the top of the stair, holding the stopwatch. "Okay," he said to Lanny, who was standing at the bottom of the stairs. "The record for running up and down stairs is thirteen hours and four minutes. Ready? Go!" Matt hit the timer. The boys started running up and down the stairs. They ran faster and faster. Matt checked the stopwatch. Only twelve hours and fifty-nine minutes to go!

Half an hour later, Mrs. McGuire rounded a corner and found Matt and Lanny lying facedown on the rug in the entryway. They were fast asleep. She wondered what was next. And what records were left?

The following afternoon, Lizzie and Miranda were sitting in a classroom full of popular dance-committee girls. On the chalkboard

Kate had lists of things that were "Lounge" and "Not Lounge." Her "Lounge" list included: Bowling shirts, Trilby hats (felt hats with a crease in the crown—GUYS ONLY), Dean Martin, and Ring-a-ding-ding. The "Not Lounge" list read: Jeans, Face glitter, Techno, Britney Spears.

"Okay, Friday's dance will officially be called 'Loungin' Around,'" Kate announced proudly. "I thought it would be really 'lounge' to have those little plastic champagne and martini glasses for punch." Kate giggled at her own use of the lingo. She picked up a wooden pointer and aimed it at a girl in the back row. "Savannah, you'll be in charge of that."

Savannah nodded and scribbled this in her notebook.

"Lizzie," Kate said, pointing at her. "Since you're the expert, we are going to need a list of the songs the DJ should play."

Lizzie smiled. "No problem," she said. She turned to Miranda and whispered, "Any idea what those songs are?" Miranda shrugged. She had no clue.

"And we are going to have a costume contest," Kate went on. "Miranda, we'll need a list of the kind of outfits the judges should be looking for."

"You got it," Miranda said confidently. She looked at Lizzie. "You know what those are?" she whispered. Lizzie shook her head.

Kate paced between the desks, tapping the pointer on the palm of her hand. "And we are going to need all of this by . . ." She spun around and slammed the pointer down on Lizzie's desk. *Whack!* Lizzie jumped. " . . . tomorrow," Kate told her.

Lizzie gulped and tried to smile. Miranda leaned over to her. "We have to get Gordo to give us the scoop on this stuff," she whispered.

"We can ask him," Lizzie told her. "But I don't think he's going to be too crazy about helping us."

"He has to!" Miranda hissed. "This is the dance committee. They can do things to us."

Lizzie looked nervously around at all the popular girls in the room. Miranda was right. Without Gordo's help, Lizzie and Miranda were destined for the "Not Lounge" list. For life.

As soon as the meeting ended, Lizzie and Miranda ran to the parking lot behind the school bleachers, where the model-airplane types liked to hang out. They spotted Gordo sitting alone in the middle of the concrete pad, tinkering with his airplane. As they hurried toward him, they had to avoid stepping on the miniature planes buzzing around their feet on the asphalt.

"Remember, Gordo's not that wild about this Rat Pack dance, so let me get around to it kind of slow, okay?" Lizzie told Miranda.

Miranda looked around at the "pilots," who were chasing after their grounded planes. "This is, like, the dorkiest hobby *ever*," she said.

"Hey, Gordo," Lizzie called out cheerfully as they walked up to him. "How's the plane stuff coming along? It looks really cool." Miranda rolled her eyes.

"I can't get the engine started," Gordo said without looking up.

"Oh, well, uh, you will," Lizzie said, trying to sound encouraging. She looked around. "So, how fast do these things fly?"

"If anybody ever gets one off the ground, I'll tell you," Gordo replied.

"We need a list of twenty Frank Sinatra tunes, pictures of the clothes people wore back then, and the Rat Pack's favorite food,"

Miranda blurted out, handing a list to Gordo. Lizzie nudged her and scowled. Miranda shrugged. "What can I say? I cut to the chase."

Gordo glanced at the list, then crumpled it into a ball and tossed it away. "The Sinatra songs were all called 'leave me alone,'" he snapped. "People used to wear 'I couldn't care less,' and their favorite food was 'good-bye.'" Gordo turned his back to them and started fiddling with his plane again.

"Gordo, come on. . . ." Lizzie pleaded.

"Come on, what?" Gordo asked, angrily. "You guys are the big Rat Pack fans here. You should know all this stuff."

"*You're* the big Rat Pack fan and *you* know it," Lizzie replied.

"Not anymore," said Gordo. "Not since you guys made it a big fad. Now I'm stuck with this lame-o hobby." He lifted his feet as a miniature jet taxied in front of him. Miranda wrinkled her nose in disgust.

"You're not stuck with it," Lizzie told him. "And you don't have to do it if you don't want to. But it's not our fault that the other kids like the music and stuff."

"It's your fault for spreading it around," Gordo said bitterly. "'Oh, Ethan, you can get Rat Pack clothes at Anteater.'"

"We can't help it if you refuse to like something just because other people like it," Miranda said.

"It's called being your own person," Gordo retorted.

"It's called being an idiot, okay?" Lizzie threw up her arms. "It's ridiculous to do some airplane thing you hate, instead of doing some Rat Pack thing that you love."

"Besides, why isn't anyone else allowed to like Frank Sinatra?" Miranda asked.

"Because they don't even really like him," Gordo cried. "They're just mindless trendoids following the herd. *I* make up my *own* mind. I'm not a superficial popularity junkie."

Lizzie glared at him. "And what? *We* are?"

Gordo shrugged. "I'm not the one helping Kate Sanders with her dance."

"No, you're not," Lizzie replied furiously. "And I'm not the one sitting here with a bunch of propeller-headed weirdos trying to get some powdered-egg-and-rubber plane off the ground. And you don't even *like* it."

Suddenly, the propeller on Gordo's plane started up. Gordo revved the engine, drowning out Lizzie's voice.

"Gordo?" Lizzie said. Gordo revved the engine again.

"Gordo!" Lizzie cried. He waved the airplane at her threateningly.

"Fine. Enjoy being a lone wolf," Lizzie said. She and Miranda stood up to leave.

"Come on, Lizzie," said Miranda. "We have a dance to plan."

Lizzie and Miranda bolted, leaving Gordo sitting all alone on the parking lot asphalt with a plane that wouldn't fly. Suddenly, two "propeller-headed weirdos" ran by, chasing their planes. *Crunch!* One of them had accidentally stepped on Gordo's yellow plane, crushing it. The kid and his friend knelt down, and immediately began to tape the airplane back together. Gordo watched them miserably, but he didn't bother helping. He hated that stupid plane, anyway.

CHAPTER FIVE

Speaking of two weirdos . . .

That afternoon, Lanny stood on the McGuires' back porch. He was holding one end of a rubber band chain as if it were the most natural thing in the world to be holding. At the other end of the chain, Matt slowly backed through the house, stretching the chain as far as it would reach.

Mr. and Mrs. McGuire sat on the couch, watching them. "I don't think they're getting in the book with this one," Mr. McGuire said. And by this point, that was a very good bet.

"Six . . . seven . . . eight," Matt counted, measuring his steps. "Eight feet! Lemme see what the record is." He turned to his mom. She held out the world record book. It was open to the Longest Rubber Band Chain entry. "Thirty *miles*!" Matt cried in disbelief. "That's insane! We're never gonna set a record!"

Boing! Without warning, the rubber band chain snapped. One half flew at Matt, stinging him in the chest. The other half flew at Lanny, who silently dropped off the side of the porch.

"Saw that one coming," Mr. McGuire commented.

Discouraged, Matt shuffled outside and sat down on the porch steps. "This is so stupid," he said. "No matter what we do, it doesn't work." Lanny popped up from beneath the porch and sat next to him. At the same time, they both placed their chins in their hands. "I know," Matt said miserably. "We're both big losers. This is our thirty-eighth try, and we've got nothin'."

"Did you just say that you've made thirty-eight record attempts?" Mrs. McGuire asked.

"Yeah." Matt sighed.

Matt's mom flipped through the world record book. "It's just as I thought," she said. "There is no record for most consecutive failed attempts!"

"Hey, you guys finally set a whole new record!" Mr. McGuire cheered. "Isn't that great, Lanny?"

"We really set a record?" Matt cried. "Lanny, we set a record!" Matt raised his fists in the air. Lanny grinned and pounded his feet on the porch steps. This was his happy dance.

"I am so proud of you boys. Aren't you, Sam?" Mrs. McGuire asked.

"You bet! You kids are American heroes," Mr. McGuire declared. "And American heroes get to go for ice cream."

"All right!" Matt shouted. "I want triple fudge!"

"And what flavor do you want, Lanny?" Mr. McGuire asked.

Lanny opened his mouth to reply.

"Lanny likes pumpkin," Matt said quickly. "Only pumpkin."

"Then, pumpkin it is!" Mrs. McGuire said and smiled at her husband. After countless attempts, it seemed they he had almost gotten Lanny to speak. She figured they all deserved a world record in the event of Keep on Trying—or at least an ice-cream cone.

Lizzie and Miranda had to hand it to those popular dance-committee girls. The Hillridge Junior High School gym was completely transformed. Kids dressed in bowling shirts or vintage suits were kickin' it and flippin' it to a jazzy number screaming from the speakers. Other cats chilled near the cardboard cutouts of palm trees, sipping punch from plastic martini glasses and otherwise oozing old-school Vegas. The "Loungin' Around" dance was an absolute total gas according to everyone.

Everyone that is, except Lizzie and Miranda. Sitting on the edge of the stage, these two tomatoes looked crushed. It wasn't like they didn't think the dance was jumping. And it certainly wasn't like they were fretting over their vintage frocks. Lizzie had on a midnight-blue sequined dress, and Miranda wore a green crepe dress with a full skirt. But while they looked like a million bucks, they weren't having a nickel's worth of fun.

That's when Ethan Craft noticed them sitting there. He sauntered over and plopped down between them. His hair was slicked back, and he was looking extra gorgeous in a blue suit and tie. "Yo, Lizzie, Miranda— awesome dance!" he exclaimed. "Coolsville."

"Right back at ya, sunshine," Miranda said unenthusiastically.

"You betcha, pally. The livin' end." Lizzie sighed.

Kate popped up from out of nowhere. It seemed to Lizzie that she always popped up from out of nowhere when Ethan was around. Not surprisingly, Kate looked great, too. Having spared her daddy no expense, she was wearing a brand-new, retro-style cream silk dress with a faux-fur stole. And her hair was teased into a perfect salon-bought bouffant beehive. Without glancing at Lizzie or Miranda, she grabbed Ethan's arm. "Let's, like, dance, Ethan," she said, pulling him away and onto the dance floor.

"I can't believe it," Miranda said to Lizzie. "I mean, Ethan Craft is noticing us. And everyone knows *we* made this dance happen. Still, I'm not having fun."

Lizzie nodded. "Me, neither. And I can't figure out why."

It's that stinkin' Gordo, that's why. He's just a dirty fink, and he's bringin' us down, just because he thinks we stole his hobby. I say we let the crybaby cry.

"You know, it's not our fault Gordo isn't here," Miranda said, as if reading Lizzie's mind.

"Yeah, you know what, if he wants to spend his valuable time flying airplanes, it's his problem," Lizzie agreed.

"I say, let's forget about him and have fun," Miranda suggested.

"Okay!" Lizzie agreed. They stood up to dance. But after a few uninspired and half-baked kicks, flips, and whips, Lizzie dropped her arms with a sigh.

"Okay. Listen," she said to Miranda. "I know this is stupid and it doesn't make sense, but I just feel like if Gordo can't enjoy this, I shouldn't, either."

"Yeah, me, too." Miranda nodded. "And it really ticks me off," she added, looking around the room. "You wanna get out of here?"

"Yeah," Lizzie said with relief. Grabbing hands, the two girls started toward the exit. But as they neared the door, they noticed a crowd gathering. Lizzie and Miranda peered around the kids in front of them, trying to see what was going on.

What was going on was Gordo. As he stepped into the scene, everyone turned to get an eyeful. From the tailored vintage tuxedo, to the Trilby hat tipped over his right eye, to the classic raincoat draped casually over his shoulders, Gordo was definitely the King of *this* Swing.

"Let's start the action!" Gordo cried.

Lizzie and Miranda stopped in their tracks. What an entrance!

Whoo-hoo!

Gordo greeted the crowd around him like a Technicolor movie star. "Hey, nice to see ya, pally," he said, patting one guy on the shoulder. "Coo-coo threads, sugar lips . . ." He chucked two girls under the chin, and continued through the crowd. "Heya, smoky, how's your Bell and Howell. . . ? Doll-face, you make me feel like spring has sprung. . . . Hey, Charley Bones, hittin' the gasoline pretty good there, aren't ya?"

Lizzie and Miranda came up and stood on either side of him, linking elbows.

"Hey, Gordo. You're . . . here," said Lizzie.

"Yeah, well, I accidentally flew my plane into the street, and it got run over by an SUV," he admitted.

"But I thought you said we were just mindless trendoids following the herd," Miranda said.

Gordo shook his head. "I never said that."

"Yes, you did," Lizzie told him. "You said this was just a stupid fad."

"Wasn't me," said Gordo. "Must've been someone else." He stepped onto the stage and snapped his fingers at the DJ, who immediately stepped out of the way.

"We were there," Lizzie reminded Gordo.

"No, you're mistaken," Gordo said seriously. Then he smiled. "You know, guys, I'm lucky enough to have friends who point out to me that I shouldn't give something up just to be different."

"Well, we're lucky enough to have a hardcore nonconformist who totally doesn't care what anybody thinks about what he likes," Lizzie said, grinning back at him.

"Good, that's settled," said Miranda. "Is it okay to have fun now?"

"Fun is what it's all about, baby," Gordo said. He picked up a record, flipped it over, and set it on the turntable. Then he held out his hands. Lizzie and Miranda each took one.

As the opening strains of his favorite platter began to scream, Gordo led Lizzie and Miranda out onto the dance floor. Lizzie spun into one of his arms. Miranda spun into the other. Everyone on the scene stopped to watch the "King of Swing" and his two best "gals" show them exactly how it was done.

GET INSIDE HER HEAD

Lizzie
McGuire

A Disney Channel Original Series

Visit Lizzie @ ZoogDisney.com

Weekends on

Disney
CHANNEL ℠

DISNEY'S
KIM POSSIBLE

SHE CAN DO ANYTHING.

A DISNEY CHANNEL ORIGINAL SERIES

© Disney

ZoogDisney.com